KiDULTHOOD

Based on the original screenplay by
NOEL CLARKE

BLOOMSBURY

First published in Great Britain in 2006 by Bloomsbury Publishing Plc
36 Soho Square, London, W1D 3QY

Based on the screenplay of the film

A CIP catalogue record of this book
is available from the British Library

ISBN 0 7475 8776 0
ISBN-13 9780747587767

Typeset by Hewer Text UK Ltd, Edinburgh
Printed in Great Britain by Clays Ltd, St Ives Plc

1 3 5 7 9 10 8 6 4 2

www.bloomsbury.com

www.kidulthood.co.uk

The paper this book is printed on is certified by the © 1996 Forest
Stewardship Council A.C. (FSC). It is ancient-forest friendly.
The printer holds FSC chain of custody SGS-COC-2061

FSC
Mixed Sources
Product group from well-managed
forests and other controlled sources

Cert no. SGS-COC-2061
www.fsc.org
© 1996 Forest Stewardship Council

1

Katie Fineal was in hell. She stood on the school playing field, barely aware of the sounds of the players and the small crowd of watchers coming from the football match. All she knew was that she hurt, both outside and inside. Fifteen years old, and her life was misery. Beaten and humiliated by Shaneek and Carleen, the leaders of the gang of girl bullies in her year at school, and no one came to her help. She was alone. Why? Was it because she was thin? Shaneek and Carleen were both big. The members of their gang were big. Maybe they hated her because she was thin. But Sophie, standing next to Katie on the playing field, was big and they hated her too. They didn't treat her as badly as they did Katie, but they beat her too sometimes, and called her a fat bitch.

Was it because she was tall? Katie hated being tall. She stood out; she couldn't hide. Everyone could see her. Everyone could target her. Shaneek, Carleen, and Sam. Vicious brutal Sam. But then Sam terrified everyone.

A shout from the football match jolted Katie and for a moment she thought there was going to be a fight and she'd get beaten up, but then she realised it was just the match. She looked around at the other kids standing near her in the cold.

Becky on her mobile. Alisa next to her. Alisa was tall, but Shaneek and Carleen didn't beat her up.

'Coming to my party?'

The voice behind her made Katie jump. She looked round. Blake, a geeky looking boy, always smiling, always trying to get in with the hard boys, was thrusting a flyer at Sophie.

'You gotta come to my party. It's gonna be heavy. Everyone's gonna be there. Mum and Dad are away, so anything goes.'

Sophie took the flyer from him. Blake thrust one in Katie's hand and then moved on, heading for the crowd around the football match. Katie saw Vinnie, Blake's pal, handing out a flyer to Becky and Alisa.

Sophie showed the flyer to Katie.

'You going?' asked Sophie.

'Don't know,' said Katie.

'Blake won't tell Sam,' said Sophie, as if reading Katie's thoughts. 'Sam'd wreck the place.'

But Carleen and Shaneek and their gang might be there, thought Katie. She'd be beaten up. Battered. Spat at. Humiliated. Where was the party in that?

●　●　●

Behind a tree, out of sight of the football match and the watching crowd, Jay stuck his tongue inside Claire's mouth, and pushed himself hard against her. But Sam could turn up any moment, so he was hurrying. Claire was Sam's girl. If Sam caught them like this, Jay was dead. Lucky Moony was nearby, keeping watch. Moony would shout if Sam came. If anyone came.

•　•　•

In the metalwork shop, Trife brought the drill bit down on the metal casing gripped firmly in the vice, one ear alert for any sound out in the corridor. Though it would be hard to hear footsteps with the sound of the drill. If anyone came, he'd tell them he was doing some extra work for his project. What was his project? A gun, man. Turning a replica into a proper working gun. He'd found out how to do it on the internet. Shit, there was how to do everything on the internet. Make a nuclear bomb. Kill someone. Do brain surgery. Make a dead gun work. Uncle Curtis would be proud of him. Uncle Curtis was a don. A badbwoy. Uncle Curtis had promised him big money if he could do this. Big opportunities. Trife was going places.

•   •   •

Out on the playing field Blake and Vinnie were working, handing out flyers and whispering 'Come to my party, blood!' to all and sundry, when Vinnie grabbed Blake's arm and jerked his head. Sam Peel and his gang of sixth formers were heading their way.

Please, no, begged Blake. Don't say Sam's found out!

Hastily he and Vinnie hid the flyers and turned and pretended to watch the match as Sam and his gang steamed their way through the crowd, barging the other kids out of the way. Katie tried to move out of their way, but wasn't fast enough. Sam grabbed her.

'Wha a Gwan batch! You seen Claire?'

Terrified, Katie mumbled something inaudible. Around them, the other kids backed away from the scene.

'What?' demanded Sam angrily.

'No,' said Katie louder, not looking at Sam.

Sam swung round on the other kids. Sophie was watching him nervously.

'What the fuck you looking at you fat bitch?' Sam stormed at her. '*You* seen Claire?'

Sophie backed away, shaking her head.

Sam spat and then stormed on, pushing Katie roughly aside as he did.

• • •

Moony stood not far from the tree, playing a football game on Jay's Gameboy. What the fuck was keeping Jay so long? Just fuck the bitch and get it over with. Did Jay think he was just his fucking security guard?

'Blood!'

Moony looked up from his Gameboy to see Trife heading towards him.

'Trife! Where you been?'

Trife shrugged airily.

'Had a couple tings to do.'

It wouldn't do to tell Moony about the gun, thought Trife. Not just yet. Later, when he was big with Uncle Curtis. When he was The Man. For now he just grinned.

'Light the zoot, blood.'

Moony gave a slight scowl.

'Just cool. Whose fucking weed is it?'

Trife shrugged.

'Exactly,' said Moony. 'Mine.'

He took the joint out of his pocket and lit it.

● ● ●

On the other side of the playing field Alisa saw Trife and Moony talking together. Trife looked like he was laughing, and she felt sick deep inside. What had he got to be happy about? Why wasn't he talking to her?

Beside her, Becky was talking.

'So I was like, listen, brush your teeth after you lick me out. Don't try kiss me after, you get me?'

Alisa nodded absently, not really listening, her

thoughts full of Trife and how they'd been together, and how he was now so distant.

'Got a spare 'grette?' asked Becky.

Alisa shook her head.

'I'm giving up,' she said.

Becky looked at the flyer for the party Vinnie
had given her.

'You comin'?' she asked Alisa.

Alisa shrugged.

'Dunno. I'm not feeling too good, and I ain't
got nothing to wear.'

Becky gave a smirk.

'If I can score some money to get something to
wear, will you come?'

'Where you gonna get that much money?' Alisa
asked suspiciously.

Becky gave a sly grin.

'Don't watch that!' she smirked again.

Alisa shrugged.

'I have to ask my mum,' she said.

Alisa looked again across at Trife and Moony,
smoking and laughing, and felt deep pain inside.

She couldn't bear this. She turned and headed back to the school building.

•　•　•

Sam stood and looked around the playing field. Where the fuck was Claire? She was supposed to be here. The rest of her year was out here. Becky and Alisa, walking back to the school building. And those two weird cunts, Katie and Sophie.

He turned and saw Carleen and Shaneek and their posse. Tough girls. Hard bitches.

'You seen Claire?' he asked.

Shaneek and Carleen shook their heads.

Across from them, Katie and Sophie were about to enter the school building, when Katie stopped and looked around. Her eyes caught Sam's for a fleeting second, before she put her head down and hurried into the building. Sam shook his head.

'Dem two girl there, they are fucking weird, blood.'

Shaneek nodded.

9

'Weird,' she agreed.

His anger at not finding Claire stirred something up inside Sam.

'And you see the way she look at you just then?' he demanded.

Shaneek bridled.

'Who?' she asked.

'Dat Katie,' said Sam, fuelling the flames. He shook his head. 'How can you let a girl like her watch you like that? I wouldn't take that, blood.'

With that, Sam walked away, leaving Carleen and Shaneek frowning angrily at one another. Then the two girls and their gang headed for the main building. Sam felt good. OK, he was upset, but someone was gonna pay for it.

● ● ●

Jay took his Gameboy back from Moony, then he, Trife and Moony headed towards the school building, the sound of the school bell calling them in. Claire had headed off in the opposite direction.

'So?' Trife demanded of Jay. 'What's her cooch saying?'

Jay put his fingers, still wet from being inside Claire's pussy, to his nose and inhaled deeply.

'Live!' he sighed. He offered his fingertips to Trife and to Moony, who sniffed. Then Jay put his fingers in his mouth and sucked and licked them.

'Mmm, taste all right, too!'

Just ahead of them they saw Alisa and Becky about to enter the school building. Alisa looked over her shoulder at the three boys, then turned abruptly away and hurried into the building. Jay frowned, puzzled.

'Trife man,' he asked, 'that Alisa is messy, blood. Why you split up with her?'

Trife shrugged awkwardly.

'I don't know man. I just dashed it.'

Jay continued to look at him, questioning. Trife shrugged again.

'She just . . . I don't know.'

Jay laughed.

'You're a fool, blood.'

• • •

Katie opened the door to her classroom and walked in. As she and Sophie headed for their desks she suddenly felt herself punched in her back, and she stumbled forward, nearly falling.

'You think you're so bad, innit!' grated a snarling voice behind her, and Katie's heart sank. Shaneek.

The next second she felt tears spring into her eyes as Shaneek's hand gripped her hair and pulled it, savagely hard.

'Didn't I tell you before? When I call you, you must come!' raged Shaneek.

Through the pain, Katie's mind was in a whirl. What had she done now to upset Shaneek?

'Beat her star!' came a shout from Carleen, and then Katie felt a sharp pain in her leg as Shaneek kicked her viciously.

Please help me, thought Katie. Somebody

please help me. She looked around at the other girls in the room, but they were turning their eyes away. Sophie. Becky. Even Alisa. Alisa who she thought liked her.

Another kick, and Katie cried out in pain.

'What did I tell you your name was?' demanded Shaneek.

'Big bird,' mumbled Katie, terrified. She couldn't understand this. What was going on? Why the names? Why these attacks?

'Leave me alone . . . please,' she begged.

The only answer was a slap across her face from Shaneek. And then another. And then a punch that sent her crashing to the floor. Pain. All was pain. She was in hell.

●　●　●

Moony wouldn't let the subject of Alisa go. As the three boys entered the school building, he shook his head and said, 'I'd never leave dat Alisa, man.'

When Trife didn't answer, Moony pushed it more.

'I'd fuck dat every day.'

'Yay, blood,' nodded Jay, joining him in the fun. 'Every day!'

Trife stopped and turned to face them, doing his best to appear cool. A cool he didn't feel. Alisa had got to him, but . . . He gave them a sneer and said aloud: 'Shut up, you pussy!'

Moony and Jay exchanged grins.

'I'd rub them titties!' chuckled Moony, rubbing his own chest slowly and sensuously.

'Rub them!' cackled Jay.

A sneering voice behind them brought them up short.

'What you uniform pussyholes know about tits and sex and dem things?'

They turned and saw Sam glaring at them, backed up by three of his crew. Jay's heart began to beat wildly in panic. Had Sam found out about him and Claire? But Jay wasn't Sam's target. Sam turned to Trife, pushing his face close to Trife's, and sneered as he said, loudly for everyone to hear, 'What you chatting 'bout Alisa for? I fucked dat bitch a few weeks ago, blood, every day for a week, when she was your girl.'

Trife could feel anger rising in him. He wanted to punch Sam, tear his head off, but he knew to even attempt it would end up with him being beaten to a pulp by Sam and his crew. Maybe badly maimed. Legs broken.

Sam stepped back and grinned and grabbed his own crotch and shook it at Trife.

'Fucked her hard, blood. Bareback. No rubbers . . . nothin'!'

That did it. The image of Sam and Alisa came up in a red mist behind Trife's eyes, and he found himself moving towards Sam, fists clenched. Immediately a gleam came into Sam's eyes and his grin widened. The excitement of violence.

'What you gonna do, pussy?' he challenged Trife.

Trife hesitated. Saw the three older boys behind Sam poised for action, fists and boots ready. Maybe knives as well, ready to be sprung from their pockets.

Then Jay stepped forward and said boldly to Sam: 'Leave us alone, blood.'

Sam turned and looked at Jay, incredulous at being talked to this way.

'Who the fuck you talking to?' he snarled. To his crew, he ordered: 'Hold this fool!'

Before Jay could move he was grabbed and held against a wall by older, stronger hands. As he did his best to struggle, Sam dipped into Jay's pocket and took out the Gameboy, while Trife and Moony looked on helplessly.

Then Sam turned to Moony.

'You!' he ordered. 'Hug him!'

Moony looked towards Jay, then back at Sam, bewildered.

'I said hug him, blood!' roared Sam, and moved towards Moony menacingly.

Moony moved to Jay and the two boys clasped their arms around each other nervously, while Trife could only stand and watch and simmer in anger. One day, he thought, I'm gonna sort you. All of you.

Sam pulled out his mobile and took a photo of

Moony and Jay hugging, while his crew laughed delightedly at the spectacle. Trife felt angry. Jay was only in this spot because he'd stood up for him. He had to stand up for Jay.

'What you doin', dred?' Trife demanded suddenly, and the sound of his voice surprised even himself. As Sam turned to glare at him, Trife continued, 'What, you can't fuck with mans your own age, you gotta trouble us?'

Sam ambled over to Trife, and then, almost casually, punched him hard in the stomach. Trife collapsed on the floor, fighting for air.

'Fucking idiot!' spat Sam dismissively.

Then he and his crew walked off.

Jay and Moony helped the grimacing Trife to his feet. Jay was furious.

'He took the fucking Gameboy, man! It's my sister's! I gotta get it back!'

Trife nodded, his whole being filled with anger and desire for vengeance against Sam.

'Well let's fucking get him then,' he said. 'I'm done with this shit.'

Just then one of the teachers appeared, glared at the boys and gestured for them to hurry up and get to their class.

'Now's not the time, blood,' muttered Moony. 'Later.'

•   •   •

In the classroom, Katie's torture continued. As the other girls looked on, Shaneek and Carleen and their gang gathered around Katie, forcing her into a corner.

'I don't know who you thought you was ignoring,' snapped Shaneek. 'Like you're something special and I'm not. You lanky bitch! No one fucking likes you, you fucking virgin fool.'

'I'm not a —' began Katie helplessly, but she was interrupted by a sigh of exasperation from Carleen, who turned to Shaneek.

'Oh my days! Didn't you tell her before, don't answer you back? She making a fool of you!'

Shaneek nodded and then suddenly punched

Katie full in the face. Blood spurted from Katie's nostrils and dripped down her face.

Katie felt tears welling up in her eyes.

'Please —' she began.

This time Shaneek's punch smacked Katie high on the forehead. She stumbled and then went down. Before she could get up, Shaneek was on her, grabbing her by her hair and banging her face on the floor. Shaneek stood up and stepped back and aimed a last kick at Katie, catching her hard in the thigh.

Katie howled out in pain and scrambled to her feet and ran for the door, her face streaming with tears of pain and humiliation, blood dripping down from her nostrils and a cut above her right eye, her thigh on fire with pain. She bumped into Trife, Jay and Moony as they came into the classroom, but pushed blindly past them.

Trife turned his attention to the classroom, where Shaneek was threatening the rest of the kids.

'None of you lot better say nothing, or you'll get the same as that bitch with her virgin self.'

Once more Trife felt anger rising at the injustice of it: Shakeen and Sam, bullies both. Everyone knew what was happening to Katie and no one did anything about it.

'She ain't no virgin,' he announced with a put-on smug grin.

Shakeen turned on him, her face fierce.

'How would you know?' she demanded.

'Cos me and her fucked the day I turned you down,' smiled Trife.

For a second he thought Shakeen was going to throw herself at him and rip his head off, but then she just sneered at him and turned on her heel. One to us, thought Trife. He turned, and his eyes made contact with Alisa, and for a second he was tempted to speak. Then he turned away from her and walked to his table.

● ● ●

The end of school and the kids poured out of the school gates like an army on the move, heading for home, heading for the streets.

As Katie reached the school gates there was a sudden flurry beside her, then she was barged and fell to the ground. She looked up to see Sam looking down at her menacingly. Out in the street she saw her father's Mercedes pull up, heard him sound the horn.

'You say anything to your dad, I fucking kill you. Understand?' said Sam, smiling.

The smile was on his mouth only for her dad's benefit. His words and the look in his eyes said it all. He would kill her.

She nodded.

Sam took her by the arm and his fingers bit deeply and painfully into her flesh as he helped her to her feet. Then he leant forward and kissed her on the lips.

'I could make tings so easy for you,' he said.

With that he released her.

Katie felt herself shrivelling inside. She was in hell. Trapped. She couldn't tell anyone. Didn't anyone see what was happening? Her parents? The teachers?

She found herself shaking as she walked to her father's car. He was finishing a conversation on his hands-free carphone as she got in. He turned to look at her.

'Boyfriend?' he asked.

'What?' asked Katie.

'The boy you were with,' said Mr Fineal. 'He kissed you.'

Katie shook her head.

'No. I fell over. He helped me up.'

Then Mr Fineal saw the marks on her face and he frowned.

'What happened to your face?'

Katie held her breath. This was her chance. Say it out loud. Have them jailed. Shaneek, Carleen, Sam, all of them. But then what? They'd be let out straight away. They always were. Katie doubted if they'd even be arrested. There'd be some excuse. Some lie, backed up by the other kids. And they'd be after her. Sam had said he'd kill her. And he would.

'Katie?' prompted her dad.

'I fell,' said Katie. 'I banged my face.'

Just then Mr Fineal's mobile rang and he took the call.

'Yes?' A look of annoyance crossed his face and he burst out angrily: 'What the fuck are you doing there? Oh for Christ's sake, that was supposed to be delivered an hour ago!'

I am in hell, thought Katie. And it'll be the same tomorrow. And the day after. And every day.

●　　●　　●

Trife walked down the street, away from school. Jay and Moony had gone their own way. Alisa had tried to grab him by the school gates, said she wanted to talk to him, but he'd got away. He had things to do. Business. He hefted his backpack on to his shoulder. Inside it was the business wrapped in a plastic bag.

Ahead of him, parked at the kerb, he saw a Jeep with blacked out windows. As he headed towards it, the driver's window wound down, and his Uncle Curtis beamed at him.

'Trevor!' he said. 'Bin waiting for you. Get in.'

Trife opened the passenger door and jumped into the Jeep. As he pulled the door shut he was aware of another man in the rear of the car.

'Business associate,' said Curtis. 'You got the ting?'

Trife nodded and opened his backpack, and took out the handgun and handed it to his uncle. Curtis inspected it, checking the barrel.

'Is it OK?' asked Trife.

Curtis gave a nod and a non-committal shrug.

'It look good, but wait till I test it.' As Trife watched, Curtis took some bullets from his pocket and loaded the gun.

'Listen, come see me tomorrow when you finish school. We can discuss business, all right?'

Trife felt a leap of joy inside. His Uncle Curtis was going to help him. He was joining the big league.

'Yeah, still!' he said, delightedly. Suddenly the feeling of delight vanished as he found himself staring the gun barrel in the face. The same gun he'd fixed. The gun that was now loaded. He felt fear. All it needed was for his uncle to squeeze the trigger . . .

Then Curtis burst out laughing and lowered the gun.

'Me just joke with ya bwoy!' he grinned.

Trife forced a grin, and nodded. But he was doing his best not to show that he was shaking as he got out of the Jeep.

• • •

At the Fineals, Mr Fineal sat at his laptop in the living room, cursing silently as he tried to work. Mrs Fineal was in the kitchen, preparing dinner. Lenny, Katie's twenty-one-year-old brother, lounged on the settee channel surfing. From above them came the sound of loud music from Katie's room. She'd gone straight there as soon as they'd arrived home from school.

Mr Fineal cursed again as he hit a wrong key, and rolled his eyes upwards at the ceiling. What a row! How could they call that music?

Upstairs in her room, Katie sat at her dressing table and looked at herself in her mirror. The bruises and cuts on her face. The tears trickling out of her eyes and rolling down her cheeks and dropping from her chin on to the notepaper on the table in front of her.

She turned her attention to the note she was writing. How could she put into words the things she wanted to say? There was so much. So much pain. So much hurt. No piece of paper was big enough to say what she was feeling. But she had to write something. She had to make them all understand what she had been through to get to this point. This dreadful dead point, where nothing mattered any more. No more sunshine. No more rain. No birds. No sounds of laughter. No more pain. No more tears.

She wrote: 'All I hear at school is that girls hate me. Sam says he wants to kill me.'

And as the words appeared on the paper, her tears dropped down on them.

Downstairs in the kitchen, Mrs Fineal checked the vegetables. Beans tonight. Beans and oven-ready chips. The sausages were already fried and warming in the oven. OK, it wasn't what those health people on the TV said they should eat, but she'd tried some of that health stuff and all she'd got was a mouthful of abuse from her husband. And Lenny had picked at it, and then gone out and got something from a burger bar. Katie had hardly touched it. But then, Katie hardly ate anything.

In her room, Katie finished the note and stood up. She looked at herself in the mirror again, and then turned and went to her wardrobe. An old-fashioned dressing gown hung inside it. Her nan had given it to her two Christmases ago. Katie never wore it, but because her nan had given it to her, she couldn't throw it away. Now she took the belt off the dressing gown from the belt-holes. She tugged at it between her hands. It was strong. But then Nan always bought good old-fashioned stuff. Hard-wearing. Her nan had told her it would last for years. The belt only had to last for a few moments. That was all it would take.

She pulled her chair across the room so that it was directly under the main loft beam. She got up on the chair.

Downstairs, Mrs Fineal turned the cooker off. Everything was ready. She looked out into the living room. Lenny was watching the TV, but from the way the sound kept changing he wasn't really watching anything properly, just channel surfing.

Her husband's expression was one of absolute concentration as he tapped on his keyboard.

From Katie's room came the thump thump thump of music. The same song, over and over again. Mrs Fineal thought about Katie and sighed, unhappily. She was sure something was wrong with Katie. She'd said to her husband she thought Katie was being bullied at school, the way she kept coming home with bruises and cuts, the way she went straight to her room whenever she arrived home from school. Or maybe she was self-harming? But he'd just dismissed it. 'She's a smart girl, she'd tell us if anything was wrong,' he'd said.

Mr Fineal looked up at the ceiling from his laptop and groaned.

'Lenny, will you get Katie to turn that shit down. She's been playing it for ages.'

Lenny shrugged and carried on flicking the keys on the TV remote, channel-surfing.

'It don't bother me,' he said.

Mrs Fineal heard this and came out of the kitchen, wiping her hands on her apron. From the hallway she called up the stairs: 'Katie! Katie!' When there was no answer, she headed up the stairs.

'Katie!' she called, and tried to open the door of Katie's room, but it was locked.

A flicker of fear went through Mrs Fineal.

She banged at the door and called out again, loudly this time: *'Katie!'* Still there was no answer.

She came back down again, puzzled. The music hammered away as loudly as ever.

Mr Fineal looked up at her quizzically as she came into the living room.

'She's locked herself in,' Mrs Fineal said. She shook her head. 'Strange, she's never done that before.'

A look of concern passed over Lenny's face, and suddenly he was off the couch and hurrying upstairs. Mr Fineal shook his head. 'I don't know what's going on, but if it makes him get up off that settee . . .' he began.

Then they heard the sound of banging and crashing from upstairs.

'He's breaking the door down!' gasped Mrs Fineal.

'What?!' said Mr Fineal, shocked. 'I only had that painted last year!'

But Mrs Fineal had hurried upstairs, a look of sudden concern on her face. Mr Fineal got up from his laptop and went after her.

Lenny was kicking at the door of Katie's room

while Mrs Fineal stood back, her eyes on the door, her hand held to her mouth in fear. Why doesn't Katie open the door? thought Mr Fineal angrily.

With a last kick from Lenny, the wood around the lock of the door shattered and the door burst open.

Lenny and his parents stumbled into the room and saw the fallen chair and Katie's legs still swinging from side to side.

Then Mrs Fineal began screaming.

It was a sound that went on and on and on . . .

2

Trife and Jay sat in Trife's room. A message had come from the school that morning telling everyone about Katie's death, and that the whole year had been given the day off as a mark of respect.

Trife shook his head, still stunned.

'Proper sad, man,' he said.

'I know, blood,' nodded Jay sombrely. 'I was about to leave my fucking drum, had my uniform on and everything . . .'

'Sam and them girls,' said Trife angrily. 'Always picking on her.'

'Yeah, but he troubles us too and we ain't committing suicide over it,' Jay pointed out.

'Was different for her,' said Trife. He added bitterly: 'If anyone should fucking die, it's him, blood.'

Jay shook his head. 'I suppose we're stronger than girls, though.' Then he grinned. 'It was live what you said, though, that you banged her. Made them bitches shut up.'

'It's true, blood,' said Trife earnestly. 'I busted her vee last year. Pussy was live!' He shook his head again, stunned. 'I can't believe someone I pressed is dead.'

'You pressed her?' echoed Jay.

Trife nodded.

'Blows! That's deep.' Then, put out at Trife having kept this from him, Jay demanded: 'Why didn't you tell me, blood?'

'She asked me not to say nothing, thought people would call her a sket.' He shook his head again. 'Blood, weird ting though, her dad come by here last night. That's how I found out she was dead. In her suicide note she said something about Sam troubling her, but how nice I was to her. He was proper sad. Then he said thanks and just bopped.'

'Rass a note,' he said. 'Did she mention me?'

Trife shook his head.

Jay looked at his friend warily.

'I never see you chat to Katie,' Jay pushed.

'Don't watch what I do man,' shrugged Trife. 'You ain't always with me. You never knew that I pressed it either.'

Now it was Jay's turn to shake his head, but in admiration.

'Blood,' he said. 'You come like a secret agent.'

●　●　●

At Alisa's house, Alisa found she couldn't stop crying. She hoped her mum would think it was because of Katie, killing herself like that, and in part it was. But the real reason lay in the pregnancy test she'd just taken. Yet another pregnancy test and yet another positive.

'I got to call Trife,' she said, feeling empty and desperate at the same time.

Becky, reclining on Alisa's bed reading a magazine, nodded absent-mindedly. Too much bother, she was thinking. Too much about dead people. Babies, ugh. Get a life!

Alisa dialled Trife's number on her mobile.

'Yo,' came Trife's voice.

'It's me,' said Alisa. 'You didn't call me.'

'No,' said Trife, his voice awkward. 'Tings. You know.'

'It's so sad,' said Alisa.

'Yeah,' said Trife.

'What you doing today?' asked Alisa.

'Gonna jam with Moons and Jay,' said Trife. 'Might go down the West End. Gotta check with my uncle later.'

'I need to talk to you,' said Alisa.

'So talk to me.'

'I'd rather see you.'

There was a pause. Then, his voice hard and edgy, Trife said, 'You don't need to see me. You're not my girl no more.'

Alisa felt the tears welling up inside her again.

She took a deep breath, then said: 'I'm preg-nant.'

There was a pause from the other end of the line, then Trife exploded: 'What the fuck you mean pregnant?' In the background Alisa heard Jay exclaim, 'Oh my lord!' and her heart sank. Now Jay knew, which meant Moony would know, which meant everyone would know.

'You can't be fucking pregnant!' ranted Trife. 'You said you were getting the morning-after pill!'

'It's not just up to girls,' came back Alisa. 'Course I'm sure. I've been taking tests all week.' She took a deep breath, then blurted out: 'Look, I want us to get back together. At least try and work this all out. I just thought you should know about the baby before I —'

'Fuck that!' came back Trife's angry voice. 'After you fucked Sam a few weeks ago?'

'What?' said Alisa, stunned.

'Yeah, he told me he barebacked you. You didn't know I knew that, did you?'

'But —' began Alisa helplessly.

'No, don't explain,' Trife cut in. 'For all I know the baby is his. Now I think about it, I'm sure it is, and *you* know that too. So fuck off!'

With that Trife hung up.

Alisa looked in disbelief at the mobile in her hand. Then she dropped it on the bed and put down her head.

'What did he say?' asked Becky.

'He's going out,' said Alisa. Bitterly, she added, 'He said that Sam told him he slept with me.'

Becky turned over a page in the magazine.

'Why didn't you tell him what happened?' she asked.

'He didn't give me a fucking chance!' snapped Alisa. 'Fuck him! And fuck this fucking baby!'

Becky laid the magazine aside.

'So, what you wanna do?'

'I wanna get fucked up and I wanna go shopping for the party tonight,' said Alisa angrily. 'That'll make me feel better. And if Trife don't want me, I'm sure someone else will.'

'I meant about the kid.'

Alisa shook her head.

'Lose it, if I'm lucky.'

Becky smiled.

'At least you're thinking straight. Now, we've got the day off, we might as well do something constructive with it. I know where we can score some live draw. And then we can go shopping.'

3

Trife, Jay and Moony were hanging. It was that kind of day. Out on the street, chatting — about Katie hanging herself, Alisa saying she was pregnant. Hanging, smoking, drinking beers, walking. And before they knew it they found themselves by a block of flats.

'Sam lives there.' Jay gestured at the flats.

The other two boys digested this information. Then Trife said, 'You wanna get the Gameboy back?'

'Oh-ho,' said Moony, in warning, shaking his head. 'Let's not be stupid!'

'Yeah,' Jay nodded to Trife.

'Good,' said Trife. 'I'm on dat. Let's go.'

'But Sam . . .' Moony started to protest.

'Sam's gonna be at school, blood,' Trife pointed out. 'Only our year got the day off, right? We can say we're his mates and we're just picking it up. Simple. Or we just ding the bell and get in the main door, then boot down his fucking front door.'

'Nah man,' Moony shook his head, worried. 'That's some police shit.'

'Look, there's three of us,' persisted Jay. 'Let's just ask for it. He'll have to give it. If he gets brave at school, we handle it together.'

'But he rolls deep, man,' protested Moony.

'Fuck it, man,' said Trife impatiently. 'Let's do it.'

The three boys headed towards the block of flats, and as they got near the door opened, and out came Sam.

'Shit!' hissed Moony.

But Sam was heading away from them, along the road.

'Quick!' whispered Trife.

Before Jay and Moony knew what was happening, Trife had hurried to the door and stopped it closing. He gestured to the other two, and they joined him in slipping through the door into the block of flats.

'Fuck, man. Sam's gonna kill us,' groaned Moony.

'He's gone, man,' said Trife confidently as they walked up the stairs towards Sam's flat.

'What if he comes back?' demanded Moony.

'He won't,' said Jay. 'What you scared for?'

'I'm not,' said Moony defensively. 'I think we should just duck, man.'

'Shut up, man. You're scared!' accused Jay.

'I'm not,' said Moony defiantly. But the shake in his voice belied his words.

By now they had reached the door of Sam's flat and Trife rang the bell. Sam's mother opened the door.

'Yes?' she asked.

'We're Sam's friends,' said Trife. 'We're here to pick something up.'

'Sam's not here,' said Mrs Peel. 'He's just gone to the shop for me.'

'Yeah, we saw him downstairs,' nodded Trife. 'He told us to come up and wait for him.'

'Oh well, you'd better come in,' said Mrs Peel. 'His room is just down the hall.'

They stepped inside the flat, and the door shut behind them.

Fuck, thought Moony. Shit and fuck. We're all gonna die.

• • •

Becky and Alisa stood outside the front door of a large old house in the expensive part of town. The style of the house, it all smelt money to Alisa.

Becky pressed the doorbell.

'Who is this guy?' Alisa asked Becky suspiciously.

'Rupert,' answered Becky. 'I met him at a rave. He's rich and he gives me weed and shit for free.'

'Free?' echoed Alisa, even more suspicious now.

She looked again at the house, and at the rest of the houses in the street.

'Who's he live with?' she asked. 'His family?'

'No,' said Becky. 'It's his own place. He's got money.'

The door opened and Rupert, an unshaven young man in his twenties, looked out at them. Then his face split into a lazy grin.

'Well, well,' he said. 'What have we here? Rebecca and friend. Do come in.'

And he showed them through the door.

● ● ●

Trife, Jay and Moony stepped into Sam's room, and stopped. Claire was sitting on the bed. A younger boy, Jon, Sam's little brother, was playing with the Gameboy. Claire and Jon both turned and saw the three boys.

'Who you?' demanded Jon indignantly.

'I'm the guy who's come for his Gameboy,' said Jay.

45

'Well you ain't gettin' it,' said Jon. Trife saw Jon was about to open his mouth to shout out to his mother, and he leapt on the boy, smothering the shout with his hand. Jay snatched the Gameboy.

'Quick, tie him up!' said Jay.

'Oh shit, oh shit, oh shit!' moaned Moony. 'What we gonna do if Sam comes back now?'

'Help us!' snapped Trife as he struggled to hold the writhing boy, while Jay set to work gagging and tying him up, with a school tie and clothes from the floor. Moony came forward and joined in.

Claire stared at the action, aghast.

'What the fuck you lot doing?' she demanded.

'Sam blasted my sister's Gameboy off me,' said Jay. 'We come to get it back.'

Claire shook her head in disbelief.

'He told me he bought that. He is such an arsehole!'

Trife shot a quick look at the clock. Sam could be on his way back.

'Come on, man,' he said to Jay. 'We got it. Let's go.'

But Jay's attention was on Claire.

'If he's an arsehole, why you with him?' he asked.

Claire shrugged.

'I don't know. He's older. More mature.'

On the floor Jon was struggling to free himself, his legs kicking out. Trife looked down at him, then at Claire.

'What's out there?' he asked, pointing at the glass door.

'Balcony,' said Claire. 'Where he stashes his weed and stuff.'

Trife gave Moony a look. The two of them hauled Jon up and dragged him out on to the balcony. Trife spotted Sam's stash, not even hidden, and scooped it up and they went back into the bedroom. Moony groaned weakly.

'You can't take his weed, man!' he protested.

'No?' said Trife, shutting the door of the balcony.

Jay and Claire were still deep in conversation.

'Sad about Katie,' said Claire.

'Yeah,' said Jay.

Moony grabbed Jay.

'Come on, Jay. Let's go!' he said urgently.

Jay shook off Moony's hand.

'Yeah, Moons, OK. Just give me a minute.'

Moony groaned and looked at Trife. Trife sighed and shook his head. Jay turned back to Claire.

'I don't know why you stay with him. You might as well be with me, dred.'

Claire dropped her head down.

'He said if I leave him he'll tell everyone that he fucked me and I was shit.'

'I bet you're not rubbish,' said Jay. 'I bet you're cold in bed.'

Claire shook her head. 'He says I'm not that good,' she said. 'I've only slept with him, so —'

Jay cut her short. 'Let me judge, star,' he said grandly. 'Has he got any rubbers?'

'In the drawer,' indicated Claire.

'No!' burst out Moony desperately. 'Not now, Jay, man! We gotta brok before he comes back, blood!'

Trife sighed and sat down.

'Just cool, Moons. Let him do his ting. Watch TV or something.'

'Sam'll be back soon!' said Moony desperately. 'His mum said he's just down the road!'

Jay had sat down on the bed next to Claire.

'You like me, don't you?' he said.

'Yeah,' Claire nodded.

'Well I like you too,' said Jay.

And he kissed her.

Claire shot a look at Trife, settling down at Sam's computer, and Moony, pacing, doing his best to keep his feeling of panic from showing.

'Maybe they should go?' said Claire.

Jay smiled and shook his head.

'Don't worry,' he said. 'It'll be cool.'

Jay helped Claire pull her knickers off, and then he reached in the drawer beside the bed and pulled out Sam's packet of rubbers.

4

Inside Rupert's large living room, Alisa sat next to Becky on the settee. Rupert lounged in a large armchair, an amused smile on his face. Another young man was sitting in the armchair next to Alisa. He smiled at Alisa. Alisa forced herself to smile back. She didn't like this. There was something wrong here.

'So, Rebecca,' said Rupert. 'Who's your lovely friend?'

'I'm Alisa.'

'Alisa,' murmured Rupert, rolling the name around his mouth slowly, as if it was a sweet. 'What a pretty name. And this is a friend of mine. Hamish, say hello to the ladies.'

'Hello,' said Hamish.

'Good,' said Rupert. 'Right, with the niceties over, what do you want this time?'

'Some weed and some Es,' answered Becky. 'And maybe some coke?'

Rupert frowned, thoughtfully.

'Hmm,' he said. 'The weed I can do for free. However, the coke and Es will cost.'

Becky shrugged.

'I ain't got no money on me,' she said.

The lazy smile reappeared on Rupert's face.

'Who needs money?' he beamed.

With that he stood up. Becky walked over to him, dropped to her knees in front of him, unzipped his flies and began sucking his dick. Alisa felt her mouth drop open and her eyes widen at the sight. Then she felt Hamish's hand creeping along her thigh. She turned. He was still smiling.

'Get your knickers off then,' he said.

Alisa felt anger boiling up inside her.

'In your fucking dreams!' she snapped back at him through gritted teeth.

Hamish stared at her, stunned.

'You're not going to let me fuck you?'

'No!' said Alisa firmly.

Hamish let this sink in for a second, then he appealed to her, 'What about a blow job then?'

'Fuck off!' said Alisa, even more firmly.

'A wank?' asked Hamish hopefully.

Alisa scowled at him.

'Keep talking and you'll get a slap,' she said.

Becky stopped sucking Rupert off and called to Alisa, 'Come on, Al! You wanna shop or what?'

'Yeah, but . . .'

'Then stop being such a boring bitch!'

With that, Becky turned her attention back to Rupert's dick.

Alisa looked at Hamish and sighed. Then she unzipped his flies and pulled out his dick. Hamish settled back into the armchair, a happy smile on his face.

'But I'm not gonna suck it!' Alisa told Hamish firmly.

• • •

In Sam's room, Jay lifted himself off Claire.

'See,' he told her, a big smile on his face. 'You're not rubbish. You're good. Look, leave this pussyhole and be my percy. I'll look after you proper.'

Claire picked up her knickers and began to pull them on.

'What if he beats me up?' she asked. 'Or tells people I'm rubbish?'

'He won't,' said Jay.

Jay pulled the rubber off his dick and dropped it in Sam's fish tank. Then he pulled his boxers and jeans up.

Trife stopped playing on the computer and stood up.

'You done? Good. Let's go you fucking One Minute Man.'

Jay glared at Trife, stung.

'Shut the fuck up!' he snapped.

'Come on!' begged Moony, and headed to the door, just as it opened and Sam walked in.

Everyone froze.

Sam was the first to speak.

'What the fuck you doing in my drum?' he demanded.

Then, through the door he saw his brother tied up and struggling out on the balcony. He gaped at that, and as he swung round he saw the used rubber floating in the fish tank. He looked at Claire, then at Jay and Moony, comprehension dawning. His expression became one of rabid anger. He snatched up his baseball bat from beside the door and hefted it in his hands.

'I'm gonna knock you two fucks out!' he snarled. Turning to Claire he added, 'Then I'm gonna shove this bat so far up your —'

That was as far as he got. There was a loud crash as Trife brought down the computer keyboard as hard as he could on the back of Sam's head. Sam toppled forward, clutching his head.

Trife threw the shattered keyboard to one side and stamped on Sam on the floor, then kicked him hard.

'Fucking idiot!' stormed Trife.

Then all three boys were kicking and stamping on Sam as hard as they could, their booted feet smashing down on Sam's ribs, his legs, his face.

Finally they stopped. Sam lay groaning on the floor, his face bloody and bruised.

'Dust, blood!' said Moony, breathing hard from the effort of stomping.

'Hold up,' said Trife. He took out his camera phone and took a picture of the battered Sam.

'Go!' he said with a triumphant smile.

Then the three boys and Claire ran out of the room, just as Mrs Peel appeared with a tray of drinks for them all. There was a crash and a scream, and then they were legging it as fast as they could.

● ● ●

Back on their home patch, Becky and Alisa walked along the street heading for Becky's house. In their bags, the two girls had the dope they'd scored from Rupert. Weed, coke and Es. It was a good score. Whatever Becky had done to Rupert's dick had put him in a really good mood.

Alisa's face still wore a look of disgust.

'I can't believe you swallowed that guy's spunk.'

'Why?' said Becky.

'I hate it,' said Alisa. 'It tastes like salty egg white.'

'With bits of jelly,' grinned Becky, and licked her lips. 'Yum!'

'But what if he's got something?'

They reached Becky's house. Becky opened the front door and the two girls went in.

'You can't catch nothing like that,' said Becky. 'The acids in your stomach will kill anything.' The two girls walked into the living room and, as Becky began to prepare the coke on the table, Becky gave Alisa a sly grin and asked: 'Did you like wanking that guy?'

'No,' said Alisa quickly. Too quickly.

'Don't lie,' said Becky. 'Did you get wet?'

Alisa hesitated, then nodded.

'Yeah, a little bit. But his ting was small.'

Becky put the coke on the mirror and began chopping lines.

'I bet you was mad wet,' she said. 'I was.'

'Then why didn't you just fuck that Rupert?' demanded Alisa. 'Then I wouldn't have had to wank that other guy.'

'You just said you liked it!' protested Becky. She added indignantly, 'Only my man gets the pussy. Unlike you, obviously. Are you sure you know whose baby it is?'

'Don't try it, Becky,' Alisa warned.

'I wouldn't have it in me,' said Becky firmly, chopping the lines of coke even finer. 'If I was you, I'd wanna rip it out with a coat hanger.' She gestured towards the magazines scattered around the living room. 'There's always abortion clinics numbers in those. Wanna bell one?'

Alisa shook her head.

'Nah, not now. Not today.' Alisa suddenly wanted to be on her own with her own hurt. 'Can I use your toilet?' she asked.

'Are you gonna do a shit?' asked Becky. 'Cos if you are, then no.'

'Yuk! That's loose,' said Alisa disgustedly. 'I don't do that in other people's houses. I just wanna piss.'

'OK,' said Becky.

Alisa left Becky chopping the lines to their finest and went to the bathroom. Inside she went to the mirror and stood looking at herself. It had all seemed so right with Trife, but it had all gone wrong. She felt like she was carrying a dead weight inside her. Not just the baby, but everything bad. Her life was over.

She thought of Katie. She'd hung herself from the rafter in her bedroom. That was how they'd found her, dangling like a broken doll. All Katie's were troubles over.

She lifted her top and eased the waist of her

trousers to expose her stomach. There it was, big and round. The baby. Suddenly she punched herself in the stomach. Then again, harder. And again. And again. And again.

5

Trife, Jay, Moony and Claire sat in the burger bar, munching on their burgers and fries, and laughed again at the picture of Sam's badly beaten face on Trife's mobile. Moony took a drag on the joint they were sharing and passed it to Jay. Claire shook her head in stunned amazement.

'I can't believe what you lot just done.'

'Fuck him, man, he deserved it,' said Trife.

'He's gonna kill me,' said Claire, and she started to shake.

'He ain't gonna do shit to you,' said Jay. 'That's my nani now. You get me?'

'Yeah,' said Trife. 'He can't fuck with us no more.'

'He's probably gonna try get us back though,' said Moony, still not completely convinced.

'Let him come, blood!' said Trife. 'See my uncle I'm checking today? He is a proper bad man. And if Sam even thinks about trying it on mans, my uncle will just murk him on the spot! Standard. In fact, we should get him again, before he can do anything to us. Just rush him, beat him up and jab his clart. Stop this shit once and for all blood. What you reckon?'

Jay gave Trife a quizzical look.

'You keep talking about this uncle that's gonna do this and that, but we ain't never even met him. Is he gonna look out for us mans too?'

'Course blood!' said Trife fervently. 'Just wait till I talk to him and you two will be safe.'

'Can we come with you?' asked Moony.

Trife shook his head. 'Nah,' he said. 'We gotta chat business.'

Jay took a draw on the zoot, let the smoke out, then said, 'You sure my man exists?'

Trife looked at Jay, puzzled.

'What you mean?'

'I mean he comes like an invisible man ting,' said Jay.

'Hollow man,' nodded Moony in agreement.

Trife scowled at them. 'I'm gonna slap you Moons! He'll be there when we need him.'

Moony nodded. 'If he's there, I'm there,' he said. 'I'll jook Sam up, blood.'

●　●　●

Alisa sat in the armchair and looked around the studio flat. They'd come here from Becky's house because Becky had said this was where they were going to get the money for their dresses for that night's party, but so far all that had happened was that Becky had gone into the bedroom with her so-called boyfriend, Mark, and Alisa had sat in this room and watched TV and eaten some of the pizza Mark had sent out for.

She could see that whoever lived here had money. Everything here showed good taste, and the money to pay for it: the pictures on the walls, the rug, the furniture, the lights, everything. But would this guy give them the money they needed to buy the dresses?

From the bedroom Alisa could hear the sounds of Becky and her boyfriend engaged in very active sex, lots of groaning and moaning and shouting, and the sound of the bed crashing against the wall.

On the table were the remains of the half-eaten pizza, an empty beer bottle, the stash of drugs that Becky and Alisa had brought with them, and two small bottles of whisky. Alisa picked up a slice of the pizza and bit into it, her eyes on the TV but her head full of Trife and the baby inside her. Suddenly, without knowing why, she snatched up one of the small bottles of whisky and stuffed it into her bag. The sounds from the bedroom had stopped and Alisa was aware of Becky coming into the room. Becky picked up a slice of the pizza.

'Now I'm hungry!' she said, smiling and chewing.

'Why did you bring me here?' demanded Alisa, feeling uncomfortable.

'We give him dope, he gives me money to buy our dresses,' said Becky.

'I didn't know he was so old,' said Alisa, lowering her voice.

'He's twenty-nine,' said Becky. 'He's an actor.'

'Twenty-nine!' echoed Alisa. 'That's nearly twice our age!'

Becky grinned and winked at Alisa as she stuffed more of the pizza into her mouth. 'He thinks I'm eighteen, though,' she said.

The sound of naked feet padding into the room behind them made them turn. Mark was standing there, in his boxers, grinning broadly.

'You want anything?' he asked.

Alisa shook her head. 'No,' she said.

Mark shrugged and cut some lines of the coke and snorted one. Becky joined him. Alisa, still buzzing from the coke she'd had at Becky's earlier, went to the table and knelt down and snorted a line too, then looked up to see Mark watching her, a look of bewilderment on his face.

'I thought you said she was pregnant?' he said to Becky.

'She is right now,' said Becky, 'but she's getting rid of it.'

Alisa jarred as she heard the words. Had she really said that?

'Ah, I see,' nodded Mark. 'I didn't know that.'

Becky pulled a face of distaste.

'Yuk,' she said. 'I can feel the spunk coming out. I'll be back in a minute.'

Becky headed for the bathroom, and Mark settled himself down on the settee and lit up a cigarette.

'You know she's only fifteen,' said Alisa.

Mark grinned, casual about it.

'Yeah, I know. I found her student card. She thinks I don't know. It's her little secret.' He blew out smoke. 'You wanna know mine?'

When Alisa didn't answer, he leant forward, winked and said: 'I'm a bastard.'

Alisa looked him firmly in the face. 'No, you're a cunt.'

Mark ignored her retort. 'Listen, when you get rid of that thing, come and see me. You and me could have real fun. Lots of great fucking.'

The sound of the toilet flushing made Mark turn his head in time to see Becky coming back in. He gestured towards the stash of drugs on the table.

'So how much you want for this stash, babe?' he asked.

'What's it worth?' asked Becky.

'Three hundred do?' he asked.

Becky and Alisa looked at one another and their eyes lit up in delight. Three hundred. That would buy good dresses for the party tonight!

'Yeah!' nodded Becky, smiling.

'Great!' said Mark.

He got up and took Becky by the hand, and then led her back towards the bedroom.

'Time for round two, babe,' he said.

●　　●　　●

It was another hour before Becky and Alisa left Mark's flat. An hour in which Alisa sat by herself and tried to watch TV while listening to Becky and Mark having sex. More screams. More grunts. More crashing of the bed.

Some boyfriend, thought Alisa. While Becky's out of the room he asks me to fuck. What a cunt. But at least they had the money. She would look so good tonight at the party. Wait till Trife saw her! But then she thought of why they had the day off, Katie's death, and it brought her down again.

After they left Mark's flat they headed for Ladbroke Grove station to catch the train to town and the big shops. As they sat waiting for the train Becky seemed wired, either from the drugs or the sex. Talking, talking. Alisa was quiet, driven down. Not that Becky seemed to notice.

'His drum was messy!' enthused Becky. 'Wish I lived in a place like that!' She put her hand to her crotch and rubbed it with a grimace. 'Ooh, I'm stinging, man. You could probably hear me.' She laughed and then made the sounds of herself having sex — panting, groaning noises — followed by another laugh. Alisa said nothing.

'So,' grinned Becky, patting her bag, 'three hundred squid babe! We'll split it down the mids. You got shoes right? We can't be looking like no tramps.'

'Yeah,' nodded Alisa.

Becky looked at Alisa, suddenly struck by the down tone in Alisa's voice.

'You looking forward to tonight?' she asked.

'I dunno . . . yeah, s'pose so,' shrugged Alisa.

'What's wrong with you?' demanded Becky.

Alisa shrugged again.

'I been thinking about stuff. Me like this. Katie hanging herself. I mean, that's really why we got the day off. Maybe we shouldn't go to the party.'

Becky stared at her friend, bewildered.

'What?' she said.

'It's like so weird,' Alisa continued. 'She was so pretty and tall. I wish I was that tall. She could've been a model. I know she got troubled, but I didn't think she would kill herself.'

'Nothing we can do now,' said Becky, and turned her attention to examining her nails.

'I could've stuck up for her,' said Alisa.

'Why didn't you?'

'I dunno.'

'Well she's dead now. Get over it. I am.' A pause, then Becky asked: 'Do you think Moony likes me?'

Alisa frowned, puzzled by this change of tack.

'I dunno,' she said.

'He's so fine,' sighed Becky, smiling. Then her face became serious. 'I won't fuck him unless he eats me out though. Do you think he will?'

'Dunno,' said Alisa. And don't care, she thought.

'When you gonna get rid of this baby?' asked Becky.

A feeling of anger welled up inside Alisa.

'Leave it, Becky,' she said firmly.

The train pulled in. As Alisa and Becky got into

the carriage and the doors began to slide shut, they were horrified to see Carleen and the gang of girl bullies were sitting opposite them. God, no! thought Becky. I don't want my face bashed up, not before the party. With a feeling of relief she took in the fact that Shaneek wasn't with them, but even with Carleen alone these girls were bad news. Becky looked out of the window of the train, doing her best not to look directly at the girls opposite, not wanting to rouse them into demanding why she was looking at them, but Carleen's belligerent voice cut like a knife through the carriage.

'St Martins girls, what you lot saying?' demanded Carleen aggressively. 'Did you hear that big bird girl committed suicide. She was proper sensitive. She got so upset when we was joking with her.'

Before Alisa knew what was happening, she'd said out loud: 'It didn't look like a joke.'

Beside her, Alisa felt Becky tense. 'Ssssh, Liss,' Becky whispered urgently, her head down.

'It was a joke star!' snapped Carleen. 'She just got a bit feisty. She needed a little slap. But we was only playing. We never made her slit her wrists.'

'She hung herself,' Alisa corrected Carleen.

Becky lowered her head further. The other girls in Carleen's gang looked at Carleen, waiting. Then Carleen shrugged and, breaking the silence, she dismissed Alisa's words.

'Whatever,' she said. 'She's dead.'

'Because of you,' said Alisa.

Carleen glared at Alisa.

'What?' she demanded. The other people in the carriage could feel the tension. Some of them buried their heads in their newspapers, others began looking at the ads high up on the walls of the carriage.

'Alisa, shut up!' whispered Becky urgently.

But Alisa didn't shut up. She looked Carleen full in the face and said: 'She killed herself because you and your friends bullied her until she couldn't take it no more. You killed her.'

'Shut up you sket!' hissed Carleen, anger rising in her face.

'You killed her,' repeated Alisa firmly and clearly.

'Fucking shut up!'

'You killed her.'

'If you don't shut up, you're gonna join her!'

By now everyone in the carriage could feel the violence in the air, knew that any second Carleen and her friends were going to launch themselves at Alisa.

'She doesn't mean it,' Becky blurted out. 'Please don't beat us up. She's pregnant.'

At these words, the other people in the carriage seemed to shrink even further back from the girls. Carleen looked at Alisa and sneered.

'Oh yeah, you're that girl that Sam fucked.' She smirked, back in control of the situation. 'You wait till I tell everyone about this ho.'

'Tell them!' snapped Alisa loudly. 'Tell them Alisa's pregnant and she's keeping the fucking baby!'

Becky turned and stared at Alisa, her mouth open in shock.

'What?' she said.

But Alisa's eyes were fully on Carleen, challenging her.

'I'm not scared of you! If you're gonna do something to me, do it. Go on then. I've got bigger things to worry about than what you can do to me!'

Carleen sat between her gang of friends at a loss. No one had ever spoken to her like this before.

'Carleen, where's Shaneek?' asked Becky.

Becky's tone was wheedling, respectful, friendly, trying to save the situation, and Carleen grabbed the chance to save face. Turning away from Alisa's fierce glare, she said, 'That dead girl —'

'Katie,' said Alisa firmly. 'Her name was Katie.'

Carleen ignored her and spoke to Becky. 'She used to do Shaneek's homework and cos of all this Shaneek's Mum found out. She was vex still, so today Shaneek couldn't come out.'

'Aren't you even sorry Katie's dead?' demanded Alisa.

Slowly Carleen turned her eyes back to Alisa, her face hard. And then she smiled.

'No,' she said. 'She's not in my family.'

Whether it was the tension of facing down Carleen, or perhaps the baby, Alisa suddenly felt nausea rising up in her. Too late to hold it back she vomited on the floor of the train, just as the train pulled into the station. Carleen and the girls sitting opposite wrinkled their faces in disgust. Hastily Becky pulled Alisa to her feet and hauled her off the train on to the platform.

Carleen and the girl bullies glared after them. Then one of the girls said to Carleen, 'You should have beat her star'. Carleen nodded. She should, otherwise word of this would get around, and where would her power be then?

'I should,' she said grimly.

Carleen got up, fists clenched and ready, but

as she was about to get out on to the platform to punch Alisa, the doors slid shut and the train began to move. Through the train window, Carleen shook her fist at Alisa. In response, Alisa gave her the finger, and Carleen gasped in shock. Then the train was gone and receding into the distance.

Becky stood next to Alisa, who was bent over, still retching.

'What the fuck were you thinking Alisa?' she asked, in amazement and outrage. 'They could've beat us up!'

'So?' demanded Alisa, and retched again.

'You're so selfish,' Becky fumed. 'What if my face got scarred or something? And what the fuck are you talking about keeping the baby? You're not going to have an abortion?'

Alisa stood up, taking deep breaths, recovering a little.

'You're only fifteen!' continued Becky. 'Don't be fucking stupid! You have to.'

'I don't *have* to do anything,' said Alisa firmly.

After taking Jay's Gameboy, Sam orders Moony to hug Jay.

Katie lies to her dad about what happened to her face.

Jay and Trife chat about Sam's part in Katie's suicide.

Yet another pregnancy test and yet another positive.

Alisa hopes she might lose the baby, if she's lucky ...

Becky knows where to score some draw and get money to go shopping.

Trife, Jay and Moony all kick Sam, their feet smashing down on him.

Jay, Moony, Trife and Claire chat about how Sam's gonna get them back.

Alisa wonders if perhaps they shouldn't go to the party.

Curtis asks Trife to come and work for him.

Trife now has his own gun.

Curtis wants Trife to handle a few things ...

Alisa hides in the darkness. / Trife realises he has to speak her.

Alisa tells Trife that her baby is his.

Moony confronts Sam at the party.

Alisa can tell something is seriously wrong with Trife.

Suddenly she doubled over and puked again. Standing up, she wiped her mouth with the back of her hand.

'I need to speak to Trife,' she said.

6

Trife was seething with fury. The day had seemed like a good one. Lots of things going for it. Beating Sam and getting the Gameboy back. Him and Jay and Moony like one. And then, as they had been walking along the street, out of nowhere Jay and Moony had started again about his Uncle Curtis. Maybe they had been joking at first but it didn't seem like a joke to Trife. Curtis was the way out for Trife. He had told Jay and Moony that as they walked along the street after leaving Claire. But Jay and Moony had hinted that there was no such person as Uncle Curtis, that it was all Trife making him up to look bad.

Angrily, he had challenged them on it, and

their argument had bounced back and forth, and then Jay had brought up Alisa and Sam. The red mist of anger had been building up inside Trife at the thought of Alisa with Sam, ever since Sam had mocked him about it. Now he burst out in anger against Jay and Moony, shouting at them, challenging them to a fight. And Moony had glared back at him.

'Don't take it out on us just cos your beans got banged by next mans!' Moony had said to him grimly. 'If you was anyone else, I would stab your clart.'

'Stab me then!' Trife had challenged him. 'My uncle will kill you, blood!'

And Jay had laughed scornfully.

'You and your fucking uncle! If my man's even real, you better go to him cos that's all you got. You ain't got no Alisa, and we ain't backing no more.'

Trife had glared at them. These were supposed to be his best ever friends, and here they were calling him a liar about his uncle, mocking him over Alisa.

'Who you fucking chatting to!' Trife had burst out angrily. 'Without me you two ain't shit! If I wanted Alisa, I could have her, but I don't need her and I don't need pussyholes like you!'

Jay and Moony had exchanged looks, and then Jay had pointed a finger at Trife and said firmly, 'You keep believing that, blood. We might call you Trife, but you're Trevor. Remember that.'

And with that Jay and Moony had turned and walked away from him.

So they were gone. Well he didn't need them. He didn't need Alisa. And they'd soon know well enough his Uncle Curtis was for real.

And so Trife had walked, his head full of so many things. Jay and Moony. Uncle Curtis. Katie. Sam. But most of all Alisa. He couldn't get her out of his head. Shit, it should be easy now. Now he knew what he knew about her and Sam. But it wasn't. It was hard. Fucking hard.

He'd walked without being aware of the direction, his head so full, but his body knew where to take him. By now it was getting dark but he knew where he was. This was the street — with its faceless buildings and converted warehouses — where Uncle Curtis had his drum. It was the kind of place that seemed to hide itself away. Perfect for Uncle Curtis's set-up. Trife rang the bell, and when the buzzer sounded, he pushed the door open and went in.

Inside the stairwell was dark. Music could be heard coming up from the basement. Trife headed downstairs.

The flat was much bigger than Trife had expected. The furniture and decoration were expensive looking. A large plasma TV was on and three women were watching it. Young men not much older than Trife stood talking in small groups, nodding and doing deals. The air was heavy with weed and heroin smoke.

Trife was suddenly aware of a smiling woman coming towards him. She looked about thirty and was covered in fake gold, and wore the shortest skirt Trife had ever seen.

'You must be Trevor,' she smiled.

'Yeah,' nodded Trife.

He felt a sense of excitement mounting, mixed with nerves. This was where he wanted to be. In the Big League.

'He'll be with you in a sec,' smiled the woman.

As if on cue, a door to a back room opened and Uncle Curtis came out. Trife was surprised to see that Lenny, Katie's older brother, was with him. Lenny looked serious and was nodding as Curtis said something to him. Lenny was holding some-thing wrapped in cloth. Curtis said something more, and Lenny nodded again, then headed for the door. As he did so, he and Trife locked eyes. Then Lenny broke it and hurried away.

Uncle Curtis came over to Trife, beaming broadly.

'Trevor,' he said. 'Wha' happen?'

'You told me to reach,' said Trife.

Curtis nodded and gestured at the woman who had greeted Trife when he entered the flat.

'You meet my woman, Debby?'

Debby nodded and smiled. Curtis leant towards

her and kissed her on the cheek, then he turned to Trife.

'Come and join me,' he said. 'Let's talk.'

Trife followed his uncle into the kitchen off the main living room. Curtis gestured at two chairs by the table. The pair of them sat down and Curtis lit up a joint.

'Me like the work you did on the gun,' nodded Curtis approvingly. 'This is for you.'

Curtis reached into his pocket and pulled out a bundle of notes, which he tossed on to the table towards Trife. Trife picked the money up, trying to appear cool but feeling a rising sense of excitement.

'It's easy blood,' he said. 'I can do dem one a day if you want . . .'

Curtis held up a hand to silence Trife.

'Don't speak, just listen,' he said.

Curtis reached into a drawer and pulled out a handgun and handed it to Trife.

'Cos you did such a good job I reckon you ought to have one of your own.'

Trife looked at the gun with a feeling of excitement and pride. He checked the chamber. It was loaded! He was The Man! Trife slipped the gun into his pocket and turned back to his uncle, opening his mouth to speak, but again Curtis held up his hand to stop him.

'All you need in this world is money, Trevor, and if you know how to get it, you laughing. You seen that big TV in my front room?'

Trife nodded.

'You got one?'

Trife shook his head.

'No. But you'd like one. Course you would. You could hook the video game and all dem ting here.' Curtis studied Trife thoughtfully, as if weighing up the evidence in front of him. Finally he nodded to himself and said, 'Why don't you come work for me?'

'I want to, blood!' burst out Trife eagerly. 'Fucking had enough of everything else. What you want me to do?'

Curtis half smiled.

'I want you to handle something for me.'

• • •

Claire was in her room lounging on the bed, not really watching TV but thinking about how the day had gone. The nightmare of the fight at Sam's flat. Jay. Did he really like her? Why had he gone off with Moony and Trife when they left the burger bar instead of with her? Was he just fooling with her?

There was a knock at her door and then it opened and her mother came in.

'Claire,' she said with a smile, 'you've got a visitor.'

Jay! Claire excitedly got up from the bed. But the figure who appeared in the doorway was Sam, glaring at her as if he could kill her with his eyes alone.

Please, no! Claire thought desperately. Don't leave us, mum! But as Sam smiled his polite smile and said 'Thank you, Mrs Parkinson' in his best and quietest voice, she knew she was lost.

'I'll leave you kids alone,' smiled Mrs Parkinson, and she went out and shut the door.

Sam turned towards Claire, the smile and politeness gone, just sheer hatred on his face.

'Bitch!' he said, his voice heavy with menace.

● ● ●

Alisa felt sick. It had all gone wrong. If only she could speak to Trife. She'd tried him on his mobile but it was switched off.

In the dress shop she'd tried again as Becky was in the changing room with yet another dress. So much for splitting right down the mids, thought Alisa bitterly. Becky was choosing between three dresses, and each of them cost two hundred and ten pounds. That meant there was just ninety left for Alisa to buy a dress. And Becky claimed to be her friend.

When Alisa had pointed out how unfair it was, and how Becky had made a promise, Becky had looked at Alisa as if she was mad.

'Who got the money?' Becky had demanded.

'I'm doing you a favour by getting you one in the first place. Soon you'll have a big fat belly so you won't be able to wear it anyway. You still got ninety quid, you can still get something nice.'

With that Becky had turned back to choosing which of the three dresses suited her best. Resigned, Alisa had found one she thought looked good for ninety. It wasn't as flash as Becky's, no way, but it would show her off tonight. Make Trife look.

Again, she'd tried Trife, but there was no answer.

So she'd rung Moony to find out where they were. Moony was always with Trife.

'The Plaza,' Moony had said.

So after they'd bought their dresses, Alisa and Becky had gone to the Plaza, but there had been no Trife. Just Moony and Jay. Becky had taken the chance to grab Moony to herself, show off her dress to him, press herself against him, so Alisa had asked Jay where Trife was, but Jay had been difficult and aggressive.

'What's up with this baby shit. Is it true?' Jay had demanded.

'Course it's true,' Alisa had said. 'Who's gonna lie about being pregnant?'

'All you do is lie,' Jay had said. 'Now you've been caught, you're trying to drag Trife back in and fuck up his life.'

There was no mistaking the venom in Jay's voice as he glared at her. Alisa dropped her eyes from his hard stare.

'Look, I think I should be talking to him, not you.'

'Well his mobile's off so there's no point in calling him,' said Jay. 'And you are talking to me. What you gonna say to him? ''I fucked another guy while I was with you. Sorry.'' He knows that already.'

'I wanna tell him the truth,' said Alisa.

Jay sneered. 'Whatever, bitch! The best thing you could do right now is fuck off and get an abortion of Sam's baby, because he won't want you and Trife don't either.'

A bolt of fear had torn through Alisa when she heard those words.

'Has he told you that?' she demanded. 'Has he told you he doesn't want me?'

'Yes,' nodded Jay. 'Now fuck off.'

Doing her best to fight back the tears she felt welling up, Alisa had called to Becky and said she was ready to go. Becky, snuggling close to Moony, had glared at her and said she wasn't ready.

'Fine,' said Alisa. 'Do what you want.'

With that Alisa had turned, pushing her way out through the crowd in the store, her eyes blinded by the tears that now poured down her face, feeling the pain deep inside. She'd lost Trife. It was all over. Gone. As she stumbled out into the street she could hear a moaning sound, like a low rumble of pain, and she realised it was coming from her.

●   ●   ●

Trife followed his uncle into the dingy room lit by one bare bulb. A man was laid out on a table tennis table, tied down by his wrists. It was the man Trife had seen in his uncle's Jeep the day before, after school. His face was bruised and there was blood on him. He looked terrified. Next to him stood a heavily built man, rubbing the knuckles of one fist with his other hand.

Curtis asked: 'Anything?'

The large man shook his head. 'Nothing,' he said.

The battered man on the table blurted out beggingly: 'Curtis . . . !'

'Shut up!' snapped Curtis.

The large man punched the man on the table hard in the face.

Curtis turned to Trife.

'See this fucker? Him take my property, but my money never come back.' Turning to the man, he demanded: 'Where the fuck is the money?'

Here, in this cold and dingy room, there was something about Uncle Curtis, about his whole manner, that made Trife shiver suddenly. It wasn't that Curtis was angry with the man for trying to rip him off, that was understandable. Man fuck you, you fuck him. It was the fact that Curtis seemed to be enjoying this. Like he wanted this man to try and cheat him, so he could catch him and beat him.

'I can get it for you!' pleaded the man. 'It's in my yard. I told you I was gonna bring it later today.'

Curtis shook his head wearily and signalled at the large man, who immediately started punching the man on the table. Curtis turned to Trife.

'What you waiting for?' he asked.

Trife hesitated, and then he joined in, punching the man, his fists hitting him in the ribs, the face. The man cried out in pain, sobbing as the punches landed. Trife and the large man stepped back and Curtis leant over the man on the table.

'Please . . . I'm sorry,' sobbed the battered man.

Curtis nodded.

But again, there was something in his nod that was more than just giving an answer. It was a nod that went with the slow smile that spread over Curtis's face. A smile that said, 'This is fun! This is what I like! I got the power.'

Suddenly a wave of misery came over Trife. He had seen that sort of expression before. On Sam's face. On the faces of Shaneek and Carleen as they beat Katie. Excitement. Joy. No, not Curtis! Curtis was his uncle! Family!

'You know what, boy. I want you to go and get my money today.'

'I will,' said the man.

'But before you go, I'm gonna make sure you remember that you don't fuck with Curtis.'

And from his pocket Curtis took a Stanley knife, which he handed to Trife.

Trife took the knife and looked at it in his hand, and then back at Curtis, uncomprehending.

'I want you to carve a C from the corner of him eye to the corner of him mouth,' he told Trife.

Trife felt his pulse race. Why him? He looked again into his uncle's eyes, and saw the look.

Curtis was enjoying this. He was enjoying the fear in the man, he was enjoying the fear he knew Trife was trying to hide.

Trife looked again at the knife in his hand, its blade sharp, and swallowed.

'Me?' he asked, trying to hide his horror.

Curtis nodded and raced a line with his finger on the side of the man's face.

'A blood cloth line from here to here.'

Trife looked down at the man's face, at those eyes filled with tears appealing to him not to do it.

'Please, no . . .' whimpered the man.

'Shut up!' snarled Curtis.

He turned to Trife.

'Come on, what you waiting for?'

Trife approached the man and held his head so he could see the flesh he had to carve. His hand holding the knife was shaking. I can't do this, he thought.

'Carve the fucking line!' Curtis's voice was harsh and commanding.

Trife trembled as he leant forward, the knife blade touching the man's skin. The man screamed and Trife hesitated, drew back.

The large man moved towards Trife, his hand reaching out to take the knife.

'No!' snapped Cutis. 'Let Trevor do it!'

The man on the table began to sob again, and Trife felt nausea rising in his throat. He couldn't stop his hand shaking. He shouldn't be doing this. Why was he doing this?

'Cut him!' ordered Curtis savagely.

Trife half-closed his eyes and pushed the blade in, felt the man's flesh part, felt and saw blood spurt out from the cut, and then he began to pull the blade, all the while the man was screaming . . . screaming . . . more blood . . . the skin ripping apart.

Suddenly Trife felt his uncle's hand gripping his, dragging the knife along, gouging deep, blood everywhere as the blade tore through flesh and then came out at the corner of the man's mouth. Trife felt sick. Weak. His head was spinning. He dropped the knife on the table. His hand was sticky with blood. The man was still screaming.

Curtis smiled at him.

'Good,' he said. He held out his arms in welcome. 'Come here,' he said.

Suddenly Trife felt overwhelmed, suffocated. He looked at his uncle and he saw Sam. Not just Sam, but all the Sams of the world. Cruel bullies, loving the cruelty they inflicted. The pain. The fear. He didn't want to be here. Ever. Blindly he pushed his uncle to one side and ran for the door, then up the stairs and out into the street night.

7

Trife ran. He didn't know where, he just ran, bumping into people in the crowded night streets. His head was full of images. The man on the table. The knife. Alisa and Sam. The row with Jay and Moony. The blood on the table. On his hands. Uncle Curtis and his arms open wide in welcome. This wasn't how it should be.

At last he stopped. He was no longer in the main streets. His run had brought him to a quiet place, by the river. He didn't know how far he'd run but his legs ached and his lungs were bursting. He slumped down on the ground, his back against a wall. The gun felt heavy in his pocket and he pulled it out. The gun that was going to make him The Man.

Trife clicked it open and spilled the bullets out of the chamber, weighed them in his hand. Then he stood up and hurled them into the river. Then he pitched the gun after them, watched it sail through the night sky, glinting in the lights on the bridge, and then splash into the river and disappear beneath the water.

I have to talk to Alisa, he thought. He pulled out his mobile and switched it on, and clicked on Alisa's name. He was about to dial when the battery signal beeped, and the phone went dead.

•　　•　　•

Alisa sprawled on the cold hard ground in the alleyway off the main road, leaning back against the brick wall, away from the hustle and bustle and the bright lights. A few yards away all was noise and lights. Traffic buzzing. People pushing. Here was darkness. Here she could hide. She put the bottle of whisky to her lips and tipped her head back, feeling the liquid run into her mouth and over her teeth and tongue, down her throat, raw and harsh and burning. She felt herself choking, but she carried on, letting it pour down, until she had to stop and cough and splutter, leaning forward to bring the dregs up and spit them out.

She was crying. She was crying so much that she wasn't even aware of it any more. She threw the whisky bottle at the alley wall, saw it shatter and bounce back in a hundred pieces, the smell of whisky raw in the night air.

Her head was spinning.

Got to get up, she thought. Got to get home.

She pushed her hand down on the pavement to give her some leverage, and felt pain in her hand. She'd put her hand on a jagged piece of glass from the broken whisky bottle. Shit!

She stumbled to her feet, and leant against the wall, holding herself up. She had to get home.

•   •   •

Trife put the coins in the phone box and dialled Alisa's number. It rang, and then answered: 'Hi, this is Alisaaaaaa. Please leave a message and I'll call you back if you're lucky.'

Trife slammed the phone down, pushed his way out of the phone box and began to run again. Only this time he knew where he was running to.

• • •

Alisa was nearly at her home, her head clearer now but her hand throbbing where the glass had cut it.

'Alisa!'

A familiar voice behind her.

She turned. It was Vinnie from school. He came over and joined her.

'You coming to Blake's party tonight?' he asked.

She shook her head.

'No,' she said. 'I'm not in the mood.'

Suddenly Vinnie spotted the state of her hand.

'Your hand's bleeding,' he said.

'Yeah. I fell,' said Alisa. 'Landed on some broken glass.'

'It looks bad,' said Vinnie. He took the bandana off his head and gently wrapped it round Alisa's wound.

'You need to get it seen to,' he said.

'I will,' said Alisa. 'I'm nearly home.'

'Listen,' said Vinnie, 'come to the party. It'll cheer you up.' He smiled. 'I promise I'll do anything I can to get you smiling.'

'Oh? How?' asked Alisa.

Vinnie reached out towards Alisa's ear, and when he held his hand out to her again he was holding a coin.

'Magic,' he said.

Alisa couldn't help but smile.

'Please, come with me,' urged Vinnie.

Alisa hesitated, then nodded.

'OK,' she said. 'Let me get changed. But I'm only hanging around with you.'

•   •   •

When Trife arrived at Blake's house, the party was in full swing. Loud music came thumping from the house. Lights were on in the garden. Blake's parents' house was big. A big drive in front. Big garden. Lots of money. Blake was a rich kid always trying to be in with street kids.

Through the windows Trife saw Jay and Moony chatting to Becky and some others. But he wasn't here to see Jay and Moony.

'Trife!'

Trife turned to see Blake standing smiling on the steps leading up to the front door. Blake was holding a bottle of rum.

'Want some of this? It's Cuban.'

Trife shook his head.

'Where's Alisa?' he asked.

Blake thought about it, tried to remember where he'd seen her last.

'I think she's in the garden.'

Trife nodded and headed round the side of the house to the back garden. Here kids were cotching, drinking, smoking, using the shadows from the trees to hide in, have sex. Then he saw them, Vinnie and Alisa against a tree, hugging and kissing, and Trife felt pain deep inside. He strode over and pulled at Vinnie's shoulder. Vinnie turned and his face registered shock as he saw who it was.

'Bruv . . . blood,' he stammered. 'I'm sorry. See you.'

With that Vinnie hurried off.

Alisa looked at Trife coldly.

'What you doing?' she demanded.

'So is he your man now?' demanded Trife.

'He's OK. He's been nice to me today. What do you want?'

'I wanted to say hello.' He saw the plaster and bandage around Alisa's hand. 'What happened to your hand?'

'It got cut,' said Alisa, and shrugged. 'It's fine.'

Trife took a deep breath.

'Look,' he said, 'can we go somewhere a bit more private?'

● ● ●

Sam strode along the night street, his baseball bat hidden beneath his jacket. So they were going to a party, eh. Trife, Jay and Moony. And Sam hadn't been invited. Well he was going anyway. Sam had stopped Claire from spreading the word by fucking her and promising her he wouldn't go, that he'd just go and see his mother was OK. Then he'd go back to her place for the night and they'd fuck all night. He'd go back to her all right, but not before he'd settled this. He'd show them what they got for ripping off Sam Peel. His fingers tightened vengefully around the handle of the baseball bat.

● ● ●

Trife and Alisa were alone in a secluded spot at the front of Blake's house. All the action was either in the house or in the back garden.

'Look,' said Trife awkwardly, 'I know you tried to talk to me before and I didn't listen, but I wanna talk now.'

'Don't worry,' said Alisa. 'I'm sorry you had to hear what you heard from Sam. And I understand that you don't want to be with me. But I want you to know that I never —'

'Wait!' said Trife, holding up a hand to stop her. 'I know you never meant to hurt me . . . blah blah blah. Before you carry on, I need to say all this stuff before I forget it.'

'I was just gonna say that —' began Alisa.

'Wait,' repeated Trife. 'What I want to say is this. I know we was only together for a couple of months, but it was fun, dred. You made me, like, feel good. Get me? Not just sex. I mean, yeah, your tings feel good, but . . . *you* . . . You know what I'm saying? But I didn't know what to do, like, when you wanted hugs and that in school. I was thinking about what the boys would say and them stupidness there. Then when I split up with you I realised I was stupid. I told them all ''I ain't going back to her'', but I was waiting for you. Then I found out that you fucked Sam, and that hurt me, blood.'

Alisa opened her mouth to say something, but Trife shook his head to stop her, and continued: 'That's why I said what I said. But I've seen some shit today that's made me think about life, and you're one of the best things in mine. So even though it's next man's baby, I want to be with you and look after you . . . both. I wanna change for you, cos . . . cos I love you.'

There was a silence between them, then Alisa said: 'I never slept with Sam.'

Trife looked at her, bewildered.

'What?' he asked.

'That's what I been trying to tell you,' said Alisa. 'He lied to everyone that I went to his house. He said I might as well go cos he was gonna tell everyone he fucked me. But he never. I swear.'

Trife looked down at her body, at the gently swelling bump, then up at her face again.

'So . . . the baby . . . ?'

'You're the only person I've slept with,' she said. 'It's yours.'

'Oh shit!' said Trife. And suddenly he was crying, all the pent-up emotion, the anger, now suddenly gone, and replaced by a feeling of relief, and love. He shook his head.

'My mum's gonna kill me,' he said, smiling between his tears.

'Mine too,' said Alisa, tears now spilling down her cheeks.

Then next moment they were in one another's arms, Trife kissing Alisa's face, hugging her close.

'We're gonna work,' said Trife. 'We'll stay together for ever.'

'I'm not sure we will,' said Alisa, but she laughed as she said it, filled with joy. 'But we're gonna have this baby, so we should try.'

Suddenly she felt Trife wrenched sharply away from her. There was a blur of movement, and then Trife was on the ground. Sam was standing over him, clutching the baseball bat in one hand.

'You pussy!' raged Sam at the fallen Trife. 'You think you bad, blood? You wanna act like a big man? I'm gonna beat you like a big man!'

With that Sam kicked the fallen Trife hard, and Trife's body convulsed.

'Where's your friends?' demanded Sam. 'You three little pussies are finished tonight.'

'Stop it Sam!' begged Alisa.

'Shut up!' Sam snapped at her, and then he brought the baseball bat down on Trife, and Trife yelled in pain.

● ● ●

Jay and Moony were standing chatting to some girls in the hallway of the house when Alisa rushed in, terrified, her scream cutting through the chat and the music of the party. 'Help!' she begged. 'Sam's outside beating up Trife!'

Immediately Jay ran out of the house. Moony hesitated, then ran after him.

●　　●　　●

Trife was curled up on the ground, Sam kicking him viciously, as Jay hurtled down the steps from the front of the house and threw himself on Sam's back. Sam threw Jay effortlessly over his shoulder and, as Jay lay there, began kicking him.

'You wanna try it on my girl, disrespect my mum, this is what you get, understand?'

By now everyone had come out of the house to watch the fight. Moony watched Sam kick his two friends, hesitated, advanced towards Sam . . . then, as Sam turned to him, he backed away again.

Sam swung round to face all of the kids watching.

'Understand, this is what you get if you ramp with me!' he shouted at them, shaking the baseball bat at them.

'Just fuck off, Sam!' The voice was Alisa's. 'Everyone knows you never fucked me!'

Sam turned to her and looked at her scornfully.

'Who would want to fuck you. Look at the state of you!'

Alisa stepped forward and slapped Sam full across the face. He stepped back in surprise, and then he hit Alisa back, full in the face.

'Don't you touch her!'

Trife had hauled himself to his feet and now stood swaying, blood on his face, but his fists clenched, fire in his eyes.

Sam sneered and hit out at Alisa again, and Trife hurled himself at Sam, the force of his attack dragging Sam to the ground, making him lose his grip on the baseball bat. Before Sam could recover Trife was beating Sam like a man possessed, his fists hammering into Sam's face, ribs, stomach. Sam squirmed and curled himself up, but Trife's fists kept hammering away at him.

'Trife! Stop, please!' came Alisa's voice.

Slowly Trife came down from his anger.

'I thought you were going to change,' begged Alisa.

Trife hesitated, then nodded. He got to his feet and turned towards Alisa. It was over.

Behind him, Sam's scrabbling fingers found the handle of the baseball bat. He lurched to his feet and stood there, breathing heavily, and he swung the bat back . . .

CRACK!!!

The pain as the baseball bat hit him was worse than anything Trife had ever known. Ribs cracked. He felt something sharp stab him inside, and he knew his lungs had gone. His heart . . .

Alisa screamed, and she and Blake ran to the fallen Trife.

Sam turned, and came face to face with Moony holding a knife pointed at him. Their eyes locked. The knife in Moony's hand shook, but Sam knew from the look in Moony's eyes that Moony wasn't going to back down this time.

'Stab him!' someone in the crowd shouted out.

Alisa knelt over Trife, sobbing. She could tell there was something seriously wrong. Blood was coming out of Trife's mouth. Out of his nostrils. Jay had joined them now, and he saw it too. He turned to the crowd and called out desperately, 'Someone call an ambulance!'

Headlights of a car approaching made everyone turn. Tyres crunched on the gravel of the drive as the car pulled to a halt, then the doors of the car opened and two hooded men got out, walked over, one pointing a gun.

'Who's Sam?!' demanded the man with the gun, his voice tense.

Sam stood there, his mind in a whirl. What the fuck was this? Who were these guys?

'Someone better start talking!' snapped the hooded man, waving the gun. 'I know he's here!'

Someone in the crowd began to cry. Sam stepped forward. 'Look, blood,' he said 'I don't know what Sam's done but he's not here . . .'

Then a voice called out from the crowd. 'He's Sam!'

It was Sophie, pointing accusingly at Sam, her face aflame with anger.

Sam turned on Sophie.

'What you talking about you fat bitch!'

But the gun pushed at his head stopped him saying any more.

'Do you know who I am, blood?' asked the hooded man.

'No,' Sam shook his head.

'You knew my little sister Katie, though, didn't you.'

And the hooded man drew off his hood, revealing the face of Lenny Fineal.

Sam shrank back from him, but Lenny moved forward, the gun still aimed at Sam's head.

'You think it was funny what you done to my sister?'

'Please man, please,' begged Sam. 'I'm sorry . . .'

Lenny pulled a piece of paper from his pocket and began to read.

'All I hear at school is that girls hate me. Sam

says he wants to kill me. So I'm gonna save them the trouble.'

He thrust the piece of paper at Sam, then snatched it back and put it in his pocket.

'There's more, but you don't fucking deserve to hear it. She was fifteen . . . and now she's gone. Where my sister was there is nothing. Just like there's gonna be nothing of you.'

'No please . . . !' begged Sam. 'Please!'

Lenny glared at Sam.

'Gimme one fucking reason you should live.'

There was a silence, and then a voice, broken and in pain and through mouthfuls of blood, said 'Because he's not worth it.'

It was Trife's voice.

Alisa looked down at Trife, at the blood that had seeped out of his mouth and nose from his punctured lungs and heart, and that now soaked her clothes, and her whole body racked with sobs. And then she saw his eyes go dead. His mouth went slack. His breathing stopped. She screamed.

'He's not breathing! Help! Help!'

In the distance they could hear the sound of sirens.

Lenny held the gun still pointed at the shaking Sam's head, then he lowered it and turned to walk away.

Sam slumped in relief.

'Pussyhole,' he muttered under his breath. But not quiet enough.

Lenny whirled round, aimed the gun at Sam, and pulled the trigger. There was the sound of an explosion and everyone screamed. Sam dropped to the ground, his hand clutching at his chest . . . but there was no hurt. No blood. No wound.

He looked up to see Lenny doubled over, holding his burnt hand. The gun had exploded and fallen to the ground and lay there, smoking.

Lenny's friend grabbed Lenny and hurried him

back to the car, pushed him in, and then jumped into the driving seat. The car hurtled away, skidding on gravel, just moments before the ambulance and the police cars pulled in to the drive.

By the front steps, Jay was shaking Trife hard, trying to wake him, but there was no waking him. Alisa held Trife's body close to her as if she could make him come alive, rocking backwards and forwards and moaning like an animal in pain.

From now on, all there was, was pain. And she knew it would be that way until her baby was born and Trife could live on.

Five years later

The gate opened and the warder ushered him out, wishing him good luck.

'I hope I never have to clap eyes on you again.'

He stepped out into the daylight, blinking at the brightness and filling his lungs with the fresh air. No longer a teen, no longer a Kidult. He'd been more than punished for what he'd done.

He looked around himself. And then Sam took his first steps towards a free adulthood.

Acknowledgements

The film makers would like to thank the Mascolo and Costa families for all their support.

Noel Clarke

Noel Clarke was born and raised in west London. At secondary school he began to excel in drama and his dream of going into acting was realised after he left university. In 2003 he was nominated for and won The Lawrence Olivier Award for 'Most Promising Newcomer'. Well known from his roles in *Dr Who* and *Auf Wiedersehen Pet*, Noel has made regular appearances on many TV shows, including *The Bill*, *Casualty*, and *Holby City*. He has had lead roles in the plays *Talking About Men* and *Where Do We Live*, among others.

Noel has been writing for many years. His screenplay for *Kidulthood* draws on experiences growing up in west London.

Jim Eldridge

Jim Eldridge worked for twelve years as a teacher before turning to full-time writing in 1987. Jim started his writing career in radio. He is the creator and writer of Radio 4's award-winning and long-running *King Street Junior*, and CBBC's sci-fi drama *Powers*. He was a key member of the writing teams on *The Ghost Hunter* and *Julia Jekyll and Harriet Hyde*. He has had over 250 TV and 250 radio scripts broadcast in the UK and across the world. Jim has also written humorous titles, graphic novels and many children's books over the years, starting in 1985 with *How To Handle Grown Ups*. More recent titles include the *Warpath* series, and *The Trenches* and *Desert Danger* in the *My Story* series. Jim was born in London. He now lives in Cumbria.

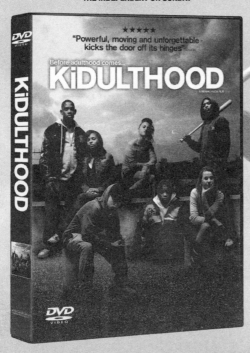